His Christmas Delivery

Holiday Hearts Book 3

By Pixie Chica

Copyright

© 2019, Pixie Chica

His Christmas Delivery
Cover Art by Pixie Chica

Thank You!

Thank you for your purchase of His Christmas Delivery. I hope you enjoy the story and will consider leaving a review or telling a friend about the book. I love hearing from readers! To keep in touch and follow my news, please visit me on social media: linktr.ee/pixiechica

His Christmas Delivery

by
Pixie Chica

Kent

With everyone around me in love, all I want for Christmas is a little love of my own. Not that I need it. No, I yearn for it.

Leaving everything behind, I'll be joining my friends at the North Pole. Hopefully, finding my purpose there. However, my life still isn't complete…until he walks in.

John

The North Pole has its advantages, but it's lonely as hell. My work for the Claus family has been my only focus. Love has always seemed unattainable, or so I thought, until I meet the new arrival.

Neither of us were expecting each other, but I'm declaring myself His Christmas Delivery.

Dedication

Prologue

~ John Alexander Jones ~

The Week Before Christmas

I'm used to waking up by myself, but doing so during the holidays makes me feel more alone than usual, especially now that the Claus twins have found their ones. They left for a few weeks and came back with their respective soulmates. I *am* happy for them, but I'd be lying if I said I wasn't a little jealous, too. I'll be thirty in a few months, and while that's still young, I'm losing hope each day of meeting my one.

Deciding not to worry, as nothing can be done now, I get up and stride toward my closet where I choose from my suits, each a carbon copy of the other, then make my way to the bathroom. Turning on the water, I let the heat of it cascade over me, hoping it can warm my soul. I love it here in the North Pole, and I remind myself I have a great life, so I shouldn't be ungrateful. I'm fully aware many have it worse.

My own mom, for example. Prior to coming to the North Pole, she struggled to raise me by herself. There were times we were practically homeless while she worked part-time as a gift wrapper. Thankfully, Genevieve Claus happened upon her and offered her a job, then and there.

After that, I grew up surrounded by love and was given the opportunity to be someone because of their generosity. Moving here gave us so much, including Tony, the man who would become the only dad I've ever known. He treats my mom like a queen. Their love is so true, anyone could see it a mile away.

I want that. The yin to my yang, as my mom loves to say. She prefers structure in life, as do I. Tony is the exact opposite. He loves to do whatever it takes to make her laugh. They complement each other, and I refuse to settle for less than that.

Once I've finished my strict morning routine, I head toward the toy shop. Things are finally getting back to normal, following the chaos that ensued while Joe and Brandie were gone. Well, except for my crew, of course.

Tony made it possible for my mom to fulfill her dream, so she now owns the local diner, *The Lounge,* though she still wraps at times to help out. I stop in and am greeted by the patrons, some wanting a handshake, others a hug. I grin and bear it. They've become my extended family over the years, but I'm not good with affection. Just another reason I'll still be single when I'm eighty.

"John Alexander, come see your mom!" I hear her shout and turn to see Crystal right behind her. They've taken a liking to each other since the latter came here with Joe, and I'm glad. My mom will never admit it because she wouldn't want to risk hurting my feelings, but I know she wanted a daughter, too. She's found the next best thing in Crystal, the soon-to-be Mrs. Santa Claus since Gregory and Genevieve retired.

"Hi, Mom, Crystal," I say, giving my mom a peck on the cheek, and Crystal a nod. Dad, rarely far from my mom, gives me a hug and asks what I'm up to. I tell him I'm off to the shop to ensure the toys are ready to go.

He gives me a pat on the shoulder, saying how proud he is of me. It may sound strange, but he always does it, and it never fails to stay with me. I grab breakfast to go and am subjected to another hug from my parents. They know how I feel about it, but they refuse to let a day go by without letting me know I'm loved.

"Can I have a word with you?" Crystal asks as I walk to the door.

"Sure. What's up?"

"My friend is moving here permanently, but I can't help him. I spoke with Joe and his parents, and they said you're the only one with a team on track. I'm hoping I can ask a favor, but only if you want to. Also, I know I've been hanging around your mom a lot. I hope that's not a problem," she blurts out, the spunky woman I met a few days ago seeming suddenly vulnerable. I'm sure there's a story behind it, but I try to keep out of people's business.

"Not at all. She's amazing. And it's nice that she has you to spend time with since I'm at the shop all day." I chuckle, adding, "I should thank you. She finally has someone who enjoys baking and cooking as much as she does. What exactly do you need me to do?"

"Grace and I are really the only family he has, and we'd like him here as soon as possible, so he isn't alone for Christmas," she begins, her smile holding a glint of mischief to it. "How does a week in Florida sound? You can help him pack at the end of it."

I don't answer immediately, preferring to take a minute to weigh my options. First, I'm reluctant to accept as I don't really trust my crew to keep on track without me. Plus, I'm a control freak and everyone knows it. The flip side to that is number two. What if they actually follow through while I'm gone? Then what'll I do with myself? But the third is clawing its way forward, reminding me I could have time to myself when I'm not helping some guy pack. I usually opt out of taking my vacation, choosing to remain behind to clean up. I want to say yes, to do something so far out of character, that I agree before I change my mind.

"I'll do it."

Chapter One

~ Kent Kayson ~

Fuck, it's hot! Wiping off the sweat dripping down my face with the towel from my pocket, I want to curse out my two best friends, Grace and Crystal. Those two witches left me all the work while they ran to the North Pole with their soulmates. That left me in charge of packing all our stuff, as well as closing down both of their businesses for the winter. The best part? I only have a week to do it.

Can you feel my sarcasm?

Apparently, I'm a miracle worker and never got the memo. *Pfft.* Add to that the couple of shifts I still work as a DJ, and this is going to be a week to remember. Yet, for those two, I'd do anything, including moving my ass all the way to the North Pole.

No one will miss me here, other than the few drag queens I work with, who have become good friends. My own parents stopped talking to me years ago, and I have no extended family. Up until the day I met the girls, three years ago, I was a loner. Now, they're all I have, and I refuse to miss out on becoming Uncle Kent when they have their own babies.

I'm still a bit shocked by all the developments. It isn't every day someone finds out the North Pole is real with Santa, reindeer, elves, and lord knows what else. In fact, Crystal's sending me one of the workshop workers to assist with the packing. My overly imaginative mind can almost picture it—an elf with pointed ears and a ridiculous outfit roaming around these parts. *Not that we haven't seen our own fair share of crazy in this town.*

I reach for the water I took out of the fridge not even thirty minutes ago and press it against my face. It's lukewarm at best, doing nothing for how overheated I am. Hoping for relief I pull off my shirt and throw it to the side. I'm in the middle of lifting the heaviest box when the pounding on the front door starts.

It's been like this all week. Unhappy clients want to know where Crystal is. It's the same over at Grace's shop. It seems every person in town has forgotten how to read since there are perfectly good signs saying *Closed For Winter* in the front of each one. Deciding it's best to just let this one go, I go about my business moving more boxes to the front.

Pound. Pound. Pound.

This time, the sound is louder, longer, almost urgent. Whoever it is, they must be on a mission to get a lashing from me because I'm about to let them have it. All my frustration comes rushing to the forefront as I storm to the door, swinging it open.

"Don't you see the fucking closed sign? It clearly says closed. C-l-o-s-e-d! As in not here, not gonna be here today, or tomorrow, not the next day…" I'm mid-rant when I finally notice who's on the receiving end of it.

Well, hello there.

The first thing I notice is his piercing blue eyes that keep me hostage for a moment. The next thing I notice is his appearance. He reeks of business and all things uptight. From the tailored suit to that neat brown hair, that's cut short with a perfectly trimmed beard to match, he's the poster child for GQ. I usually can't stand men like him. They're always so full of prudish attitudes, looking down on others. It's my mission to stay away from men like this one. Which only makes me angry that he's affecting me as much as he is.

"Sorry, I, ah… I didn't mean to bother you. Crystal Sugarplum sent me here. Maybe, I'm in the wrong place," he says in a gravelly, low voice, stepping back to look at the number on the door.

This is my helper? Since when did tall, devastatingly handsome men become Santa's elves? The stories have fooled us all.

"No, you're in the right place. Um…come in. I wasn't expecting you just yet, and not anyone who looks like you, that's for sure." I mumble the last part, opening the door to let him through, and his subtle, expensive cologne hits me.

Holy fuck, yeah, this man is not a damn elf.

"What exactly were you expecting?" He stops midstride, turning to face me.

"You know. Pointy ears, pointy shoes, dressed in a green or red felt outfit," I admit, feeling a blush creep up. I'm not one to embarrass easily, but I just stereotyped Mr. Gorgeous-and-knows-it.

"Sorry to disappoint, Santa Claus demands the college graduates wear formal wear. Unfortunately, I had to give up the jolly good outfit. As for the ears, well they retract when I'm out in public."

"Really? Can I see? And is it like a real elf university?"

Amused with my response, he lets out a full-blown laugh that's so rich I want to hear it again. Only then do I realize he's pulling my chain. Pissed off, I walk away, not bothering to show him the way. Of course, he's hot on my trail, and I want to punch him in the throat or maybe his face, so he could be less attractive. Or more, considering he might look like a badass.

"Hey, hey, wait. Listen, I was just messing around. I don't get to meet a lot of people who know about us. It was cute to see you believe my bullshit."

That stops me in my tracks. He stumbles into me and has to take a few quick steps back to not fall over. "Cute? I'm a fucking thirty-year-old man, who can more than likely kick your ass. There's nothing cute about me. I don't enjoy getting made fun of by men like you. Men who think they're are better than everyone else in the room. I know your kind."

My words shock him making me feel bad when his demeanor changes. He goes quiet and stares at the ground.

"I apologize. I…I shouldn't have done that. I'm not great with people, and I don't even know why I let Crystal convince me to come. I'm better off in my office where people are used to my awkwardness. Fucking knew this would happen," he says in an almost whisper.

"It's fine. I'm sorry I blew up. I'm not great at reading people, either. Crystal's family are all suits, as my own father is. None of them are great examples, but we'll have to co-exist, so let's start over. I'm Kent Kayson." I extend my hand, and he takes it, shaking it.

"John Alexander Jones."

Shit, this is the single guy Brandie talked about. The current of electricity that courses through me at his touch makes me drop his hand abruptly. Our eyes meet as silence falls between us.

Did he feel it, too?

Chapter Two

~ John Alexander ~

I wasn't expecting my future when I knocked on the door. That's exactly what I found when I looked at him. That spark of magic I knew all too well from those that experience it at the North Pole. However, now that I found it in Kent, I need him to know it. I'm just not sure how I'm going to accomplish that. I already messed up the first impression because I was so amused at his innocent questioning. Just as I'd predicted, when I met the one, I messed up royally. Kent already had a predetermined hatred of all men who wear suits, which sucks because I wear them ninety-nine percent of the time.

The first thing on my agenda is getting a new outfit that doesn't remind him of how much he wants to eliminate my kind from his life. Then, I need to learn how to actually talk to people. I'm horrible at it, but I desire to do so with him.

From the moment we shook hands, it was as if a magnet pulled me to him. I want, no, *need* to know what it feels like to hold him in my arms or to walk down the street, his hand in mine. The yearning to do this willingly is new to me. The few boyfriends I had in the past always told me I was cold or distant. Which I admit is true. Looking back, not a single one instilled these feelings in me, even after dating them for months.

Looking over at Kent, trying not to get caught staring when he bends to move a machine, I groan.

He's got a nice ass.

My pants start to strangle me, and I adjust myself, hoping the jacket covers my damn hard on. Now, I'll have to wear this all day.

Kent looks like a model with his tanned skin and caramel eyes. I watch as he lifts another box and a drop of sweat runs down his broad back, and not for the first time today, I wonder what it would feel like to lick it off him.

That should have all kinds of warning bells going off about the state of my mind, but it doesn't. He's strong but not built like some men who are all bulgy muscles. He's more the athletic and lean type. Even his height is perfect, being just a couple inches shorter than my own six feet. I'd love to push him against a wall as I pull on his long hair and bite his neck. The feel of his scruffy beard against my own would be heavenly.

Fuck me, I'm going to be sporting a wet spot.

He turns around with a questioning look, and I realize I've said the words out loud. I can only hope he didn't hear me, and I get back to work. Hours go by where we get most of everything packed. I finally get him to loosen up enough to accept having dinner with me — sort of. He accepts picking up pizza and bringing it back to the shop. But I'm counting it as a date. I've got to take all the advantages I can.

* * * *

Sitting cross-legged in front of me, leaning back on his elbows, Kent throws his head back in a burst of genuine laughter. The sound is the sweetest thing I've ever heard. The inclination to kiss him is so strong, I'm not sure I can contain myself much longer. *Tomorrow.* I have to find a way to get him to let me kiss him by then or I'll go crazy.

"Okay, so tell me, what's the worst thing about you?" he asks with a glint of honest curiosity in his eyes.

"I don't 'people' well," I admit. "I often say things others don't take quite right. Case in point, our earlier interaction. I also struggle with being affectionate."

"That can't be good for your boyfriend," he tells me, having already established we're both gay.

"No boyfriend. It's been a while, unless you consider work my man. It keeps me up at all hours of the night." I laugh, but there's so much truth in that statement.

"Oh, so you're one of those. A workaholic," he says, and the words sound like poison coming out of his mouth, his eyes darkening with the statement. Craving to see his smile again, I lie and hope I can deliver on it when the time comes.

"It's just something I do to pass the time. It's not like there's someone waiting for me at home." I shrug.

"Okay, I guess I get that."

Deciding I have to put all the cards on the table, I bite my lip, second-guessing myself. *Will I be okay with him rejecting me?* No, I won't, but I still have to try. If he refuses, I'll just keep trying until he realizes we're meant to be. It's destiny, the proof beating in my chest. I've never felt like this just from looking at someone, and I won't let go of that.

"Something on your mind?" he asks, reading right through me.

Clearing my throat, I ask him out.

He stares at me until I start to get nervous. The way his eyes bore into me is almost like he's seeking to find all my secrets to dissect them one by one. And I'd let him for a chance at forever with him. The thought hits me like a bucket of cold water.

Do I really want forever? Yes, desperately.

"You're going to make this hard on me. I can tell."

"Make what hard on you?" I ask.

"You don't want to know how many things."

I watch his Adam's apple move up and down as he swallows. His words mean so much more, the sexual tension between us thick in the air.

"You still didn't answer my question."

"I know."

Sadly, the moment is lost when someone knocks on the door, both of us cursing when it happens. I almost had him agreeing to a date, before the super of the building who's now on my shit list, came interrupting. After getting some things settled with Kent, he leaves, but there's no way to go back to that magical moment we just shared.

Coming toward me, Kent extends his hand out, helping me up. I take it, dusting the dirt from the floor from my pants, which isn't much.

"So…I better get going," he says. "Your hotel isn't too far from my apartment. I can give you a tour of the town before we finish packing if you'd like. Crystal texted me where you are staying earlier. I can come by to pick you up, if you'd like."

Not about to look a gift horse in the mouth, I accept the tour. Any time I get to spend with him is a plus in my book. Stepping outside, he locks the door and goes in for a handshake, but of course, I misread going in for a hug. We end up doing this weird shake-hug combo, and I want to bang my head against the wall. The only good thing is it makes him smile. Happiness fills me for the first time ever, as I walk toward the car.

After finding an outfit at the nearest clothing store that looks as casual as I can pull off, I head to my hotel to try to get some sleep. Only, it doesn't come. I'm too excited about our tour tomorrow. I pace the room then head outside to go for a walk. By the time I make it back to my hotel, it's five in the morning, so I jump in the shower.

Looking at my phone after getting dressed, I see a text from Crystal. My luck seems to be getting better by the minute. The woman is a lifesaver. She let me know where the spare key is, as well as inviting me to make myself at home. With renewed energy, I head toward the apartment. What's the worst that could happen? I kind of like this living on the edge stuff.

Chapter Three

~ Kent ~

Waking up with no one else in the apartment is nice for a change. Although I loved living with Crystal, there's a freedom in knowing I can walk around my house naked while singing off-key. Sitting up in bed, I glance at the clock and realize it's too fucking early to be awake, but I know I must go back to packing.

Yesterday, we finished most of it, way ahead of schedule, and I'll be glad to cross that off my checklist. Not to mention, I'm supposed to play tour guide for John Alexander, and that will prove to be hard as fuck to do. Especially since he broke through my defenses. I'd been so close to agreeing to go on a date with him. The easy banter and conversation between us had felt natural. Then his small half-smiles and hearty laughter had me wanting to forget all about avoiding men like him.

Since we got interrupted, I went home. Sometime, late last night, Crystal called in an effort to calm her nerves and make sure I'm still coming. I could tell she was having a hard time assimilating to everything, and she wanted someone to hear her out. She's especially nervous about Joe going solo around the world, having big shoes to fill, and that's scary enough. But, like me, she's leaving everything behind for a world we thought only existed in books and little kid's imaginations.

Determining it's best to get a head start today and have some coffee before dealing with the man I developed an unhealthy crush on within hours of meeting, I hit the alarm before it sounds. Taking my newfound liberty and self-indulgent attitude in full swing, I let it all hang out. After doing my morning hygiene routine, I head for the kitchen to grab my protein shake. I hate that shit, but it's a habit Crystal got me into. According to her, I need to live forever to keep her company. After gulping it down, I grimace then go to my TV for my daily meditating.

"Okay, self, it's time to get a head start on your New Year's resolutions. Let's get these stretches in. Alexa, play the instrumental playlist." Heading to the empty space, I lay out my exercise mat and let the music drown all my emotions. Sitting Indian style, I start my affirmations, another of Crystals must-do's. "I will be awesome today. I will own it and claim it as Kent's Day. No one will cause me to get distracted. Especially not the hot Christmas elf in the suit."

I'm feeling on top of the world and pretty good about getting my head on straight when I hear the clearing of a throat. Getting on my feet faster than I ever have in my life, I come face-to-face with none other than John.

A blush creeps up my cheeks when he doesn't avert his eyes. He's trying hard to hide the smile creeping up the sides of his mouth. "So, is it safe to say you still think I'm an elf?" he asks.

This time, he does smile and it lights up his whole face, making him even more desirable. When I glare at him, he changes his tune.

"Okay, I'll skip that question. Crystal gave me the spare key, so I let myself in. I figured you'd like some company and some strong coffee. Are you a nudist? I don't think we've had one of those before, but as long as you do it inside your home, you'll be fine."

"What? Nudist? Jeez, no! I was just…" It's then I realize I've been naked this whole time, too distracted to notice before. "Never mind what I was doing. Why are you at my house at six a.m.?" I yell, grabbing a throw pillow off the sofa to cover my junk. Appalled at the turn of events, I run to my room to put on some pants.

"This is late for me. I'm always up at four a.m., but I couldn't sleep last night. Nice package by the way!"

Nice package? This guy has to be mental.

Emerging from my room a few minutes later, fully dressed and with extra layers on, I'm ready to take on John. He's leaning against the wall, looking at his phone, giving me a minute to take him in. Damn, today is going to be torture. He's exchanged his suit for jeans and a Christmas shirt that's tight against his arms and chest. He's even more fit than I assumed yesterday. My wandering eyes dare to go lower, and I aim right at his tented pants. *Oh!* Averting my eyes the second I do it, I look up and find I've been caught.

"Just so you know…I don't mind being your Christmas Elf," he says, pushing off the wall.

"How about that tour?" I reply, trying to change the subject, but he doesn't let me.

"How distracted do I make you?"

"You heard all of it, didn't you?"

"Yup, and I can't say I'm mad about it. But I guess we can go on that tour; I'd love to get to know you better before you go out to dinner with me."

"That's a little presumptuous, don't you think? I never said yes yesterday. Why would I now?"

"Because you were about to say yes yesterday. You said it yourself, I'm a distraction.

Why not see if that's all I am? Then you can move on to the *Year of Kent*, or not." He wraps an arm around my shoulder before continuing. "I rather it be the year of Kent and John."

"Fine, I'll take you up on that dinner, just so I can find your flaws and run."

"We'll see what happens. I have no clue why Crystal picked me, but I'm thanking my lucky stars she did. I've got plans for you and me." He winks at me, and I scoff at him.

"What plans?"

"You'll see."

"Whatever. Let's get this tour on the way." I try to remove his arm, but he only pulls me closer, and I let him, finally giving up on eradicating his tight hold.

"And dinner. Let's not forget that."

* * * *

When something is too good to be true, trust your instincts.

Mr. Perfect has a huge flaw. One I saw coming, although he'd denied it through and through. We were having a swell time when his job called in the middle of an early dinner, which we had planned to follow with a movie. I told him it was fine, but one phone call turned into twenty, and the next thing I knew, he set up a makeshift office in my apartment. Laptop, mini printer, the whole works, and all the while the man didn't even acknowledge I was in the room.

Don't get me wrong. I wasn't pissed because there was an emergency. I understood things happened, but he went from damage control to full-on control freak, drilling everyone in his team.

I know what it is to work all the time — hell, I work three different jobs, but I also know when to quit. In lieu of sitting there watching him turn into the boss from hell, I took an extra shift at Sashay Queens and came back hours later to find him in the same spot. He looked tense and stressed, and a part of me hurt for him.

Determined not to judge the guy by one day's actions, I walk out this morning, ready to invite him to the brunch show I Deejay on Sundays. Maybe after we can finish the last bit of packing. Only, he's in the same spot, phone in hand, and definitely wearing yesterday's clothes.

Not bothering to say goodbye, I leave, placing a note on the door for him. When he comes out of zombie mode, he can find me, if need be. I know his kind, and I want nothing to do with it. He blew his chance. Yet, the knowledge upsets me, and I'm a mess.

My father was a workaholic, and he drove my mother into alcoholism. Growing up, it killed me to see her drink her way into oblivion night after night. I haven't seen her in years, but I'd bet my last dollar she's drunk right now. Or maybe, she finally let the bottle take her to the grave. When I left home, years ago, I begged her to come with me, which only earned me a slap. She even went as far as to banish me, asking that I never come back. Her infatuation with him blinded her. Not once did she see how his cold indifference destroyed the joyful woman she'd once been. *Yeah, no thank you.*

Pushing John from my head, forgetting that yesterday he gave me more emotions in a matter of hours than any of my few exes put together, I concentrate on my set. I'm in the middle of one of my favorite playlists, lost in the music, when Tim, one of my co-workers, comes into the booth with me. He reaches over to grab something, and he gets a little too close, so I move to the side. When he leaves, I find his action odd. He knows how much I avoid him. We went on one date when he wouldn't stop insisting, and I ran the other way.

At the end of my set, I take a break from Deejaying, and Olivia Lightning Fuck, one of the headlining Drag Queens, comes my way. There's a funny smile on her face, and I cock an eyebrow at her.

"You naughty, naughty Kent. No wonder you never let anyone hit on you. If I had a man like that at home, I'd be keeping all the idiots at bay, too. Can't believe how well you kept that a secret."

Not quite sure what she's talking about, I ask her to clarify. When she points in the direction of one of the tables, my heart stops. There, in a corner booth, is John, back in business attire, but he doesn't look as put together as he did that first night. His shirt sleeves are rolled up, and there are a few loose buttons, putting me on alert that something is wrong. It's his look of distress that concerns me the most.

"Your boyfriend requested three times that I please call you down when you were done. What did you do? Leave home without giving him his morning biscuit?" she teases, giving me a wink. "He's about to lose it waiting for you."

"Shut up. He's not my boyfriend," I reply.

"No, you're right. The way he worded it was he's your man. So um…you better get on that." She walks away laughing. *My man? What the fuck?*

Chapter Four

~ John Alexander ~

I fucked up. I knew it, and when I heard the front door close with a bit of a slam, it knocked me right on my dumb ass. My controlling self had gone to work and stayed up all night over something that would have worked itself out. I promised Kent dinner and a movie, and what did I do? I barely made it through dinner, when I answered what should have been a quick phone call, and it turned into me becoming work-obsessed.

But no more. I wasn't ruining the small chance he gave me. Taking the note he'd left behind, being extra thankful he wasn't mad enough not to tell me where he'd be, I get ready to head out the door. Until I look down and see I'm still in yesterday's clothes.

Yeah, you're an idiot.

I make quick work of a shower then put on all I have left, another suit.

Great, John, let's head there in the damn outfit he hates.

I could already hear him venting to Crystal about the stiff she sent over. Half of me wanted to find something else to wear, so I'd have one less thing against me, but that would mean wasting more time I didn't have.

Making it there in minutes, I realize he works at a drag show. Walking in, it hits me how little I know about him. Something I'm going to change quickly. I get seated by a very tall queen. Her top says, Jessica Rabid, and it fits. A post-apocalyptic version of the popular cartoon who takes her character seriously, she limps over, head cocked to the side in true zombie fashion.

As soon as I tell her who I'm looking for, the act falls momentarily and she perks up, looking surprised. Guiding me to a corner table, she hands me a menu. When she leaves, I scan the area and find Kent in an open DJ booth and just the sight of him has me wanting to run up there to kiss him. It's clear people come here for the show, but there's plenty staring his way like he's the next snack. But fuck that, if he's going to be anyone's snack, he's going to be mine.

Clenching my fist, this overly tanned idiot comes to my table, blocking my view. "You sure you're in the right place? You didn't get lost on the way in, or are you one of those men that come here thinking they can get a quickie then go back to their straight life?"

"Neither, asshole. I am waiting on my man. Do you mind?" I say, pointing to the DJ booth.

"Kent? You want me to believe he'd date someone like you?"

"Not fucking dating. He's about to be my fiancé."

The guy, who's name tag says Tim, gets infuriated at my comment, and I can almost see the steam emanating from his skull.

"That's fucking impossible. You're just some rebound, and that's all you're going to be. I dumped him, and I can have him back anytime I want."

"Bullshit."

Ready to go off on this idiot, who's trying to claim what's now mine, I get up to give him a lesson. A different drag queen comes over to figure out what's going on, and before I can explain, Tim lies, saying everything is fine before walking away. I'm unsure what he's up to, but I can see the intention in his eyes. This fucker is about to cause problems. *Well, I'm ready.*

I politely tell the new Queen, Olivia, about needing to see Kent, and she gives me the same amused look as Jessica did earlier.

Could it be he really did have some relationship with Tim, and I am a rebound? *Too bad, because I'm going to rebound myself into marrying him. That's for sure.* Tapping my foot incessantly, I ask Olivia twice more for her to make sure Kent gets the message. Unable to do anything until he's finished, I sit and stare at him.

I'm in awe of how talented he is, and I admire how he does everything with such passion. From the short conversations we've had, I've learned he's a great sport for anything, and I can see our life will definitely be fun. It doesn't hurt that the man is sexy as all hell, and let's just say he's packing. I'm mid-fantasy of him on my bed when Cheeto-head walks up the steps and into the booth. I almost get up from my chair and ransack him when he gets super close to my Kent, but Olivia stops me. She shakes her head and promises to bring him down in a few minutes. By the time I hear Kent announcing his break, I'm about ready to pull him out.

"What the hell are you doing here? I thought you were working. And what's this bit about you calling yourself my man?" Kent says, pissed off.

Get used to it because I'm not going anywhere.

"I came to apologize and tell you I was an ass. Come to find out, I'm just some rebound. Too bad, I refuse to be only that."

"What the hell are you talking about? Look, you can leave. I can get the rest of my packing done. I got the number from Crystal for the movers you all use. They can put my shit in the truck," he says, putting his hands in his pockets and turning to walk away. His leaving propels me into action. I grab his arm and pull him back toward me.

"Where do you think you're going? You lead me on, making me think there can be something between us, and now, you're just *okay bye*?"

"Look, leave me alone, John. I got the message loud and clear last night. I think you're cool and all, but I know your type. You're married to your job and always will be. I can't live that life. What else do you fucking want from me?"

The club has stopped looking at the show. Instead, they are fully engrossed in our conversation. Even the drag queen performing stopped mid lip sync. I've never been comfortable having eyes on me, but for him, I'll face all my issues.

"I want you to admit I'm not a rebound. That you feel something for me because I'm gone for you. I've never felt this way, and shit, I know it's fast, but

I can't help it. I need to know, is Tim just some guy you dated? Or was he the love of your life, and I just found you too late?"

"What?"

"I know all about your ex, Tim. He came over here, telling me you weren't over him, but you know what? I don't fucking care. I'll take being your rebound. I'll be the guy who came after the love of your life. I don't even need you to tell me. I'm giving my two weeks' notice as soon as we get back. I'll work part-time at *The Lounge* just to prove your happiness is all that matters," I say all at once.

"John, stop. That's not it," he says, covering my mouth, but I push his hand away.

"Let me finish. You're mine. Fuck that guy! He didn't love you enough, but I do. The minute I heard the door slam, I realized how foolish I'd been. I won't ever take you for granted again. I came straight here. That's got to count for something. I know I'm not perfect, and I can't guarantee you won't get mad at me again. I'm hot-headed, bossy, and probably all the wrong damn things for you, but I can't see myself with anyone else. So…"

My heart thumps so loudly, it feels like the whole room can hear it. Falling on one knee, my hand shaking, I take his in mine. "Kent, we're getting married. You can pick the day, you can pick how, but we're not leaving this place without you agreeing. I don't have a ring, but as soon as we get out of here, we can go get one. I tried to think of all the possible outcomes that involved me walking away. Not a single one is doable. So, there's only one plan. Making you love me."

"You crazy man, I already do! Tim was never a thing."

He pulls me up to my feet. Wrapping his arms around me, we kiss, our tongues dancing together, neither of us wanting to stop. I feel him in every part of me. He's the man I never knew I was waiting for. The kiss we share is sweet, but passionate, much like Kent, and I can't get enough. When it ends, I can't help but smile. Calm falls over me, and all the anxiousness I'd felt dissipates, although my hands still shake.

"Here, in front of everyone as our witnesses, I'm saying yes to you because you stole my heart with just one look, melted me with just one smile. That first day, I wanted nothing to do with you and your damn suit and what I thought would be a rigid man with no emotions. Hell, I gave up when you ignored me all night, but you just kissed me in the middle of this bar. I know that wasn't easy for you. However, if you even once pull that shit again, you'll be in the literal doghouse."

"Deal!"

Once everyone calms down with their applause, we sit together in the same booth. I have him sit right next to me, even if some think it's tacky. I need to be close to him and feel like this is real. We're mid-brunch when his earlier words strike me.

"Wait, when you said Tim was never a thing, what did you mean?" I ask. "Didn't you love him? Not that it matters, but it would make me feel a bit better, seeing as you're the first man I've ever loved.

"Exactly what I meant. Tim was never a thing. He asked me out once. I did the polite thing and accepted then excused myself, telling him it wasn't going to happen. I've dated, but never once felt what I feel for you. I have to say, you all are fast movers up in the North Pole, three for three. I was determined to be single next year. It was supposed to be the Year of Kent."

Looking down into his eyes, I kiss his lips softly. "I think the year of Kent and John sounds much better."

"Aren't you just the charmer?"

"Only with you."

* * * *

December 26th

The girls are waiting for us outside the trolley as we make our way to the front. They don't know I'm arriving not only with Kent, but engaged. As it comes to a stop, I tell him to stand back for a second, so I can surprise them.

"There you are! Took you long enough. Where's my Kent? You didn't hurt him, did you? I like you, but I will stab you in the dick!" Crystal says, pushing past me and going up to the bus. I head over to Brandie, excited to hug my friend, who's just as thrilled to see me.

"Listen, I heard all about John being an uptight prick, so I got margaritas at my house, and it was a surprise, but what the heck, I got you a stripper," Crystal says, glaring at me like I did something wrong. Kent still messing with her.

At the mention of strippers, my eyes go wide. *Oh no.* "Um…I hope that stripper is for one of you ladies because he's taken." When he stands next to me, I lay a possessive arm around him.

"Oh my god, you guys really did get together! I knew it! I knew it, knew it, knew it! Pay up, buttercup!" Grace says to the other two, who roll their eyes and pull twenty-dollar bills from their pockets.

"Are you serious? You were betting on whether we made it or not? I'm appalled." I act shocked, but I'm really not.

"Yeah, and I'm out twenty bucks. Fucking A. I swear John, the one time I need you to be your anti-people self, you falter," Brandie replies.

"So, when did you guys become official?" Crystals asks before continuing, "Because I never thought you'd find a boyfriend after your 'I'm living for me and only me' Kent speech."

"Fiancé, not boyfriend. I slid right into forever mode. He won't be able to get rid of me now." I inform them, showing them our matching rings.

Chapter Five

~ Kent ~

New Year's Eve

Damning myself for getting out so late, I make a sprint to the house. If I don't hurry, I'll miss the call from John, my phone being dead and all. He's gone with Joe to do some damage control at one of the toy-making companies threatening to pull their contract. Not even two weeks ago, I chastised him for working late, and here I am doing the same. But I get it. Once you become part of the Claus family, it's more than a job. The need to be part of bringing joy to the world is unlike anything else. Within days of being here, I was fully committed to being part of the mission. I went from working in the toy shop to manager, and now I'm engrossed in everything.

That doesn't mean I won't hear it from John, who tried to tell me this would happen. Making it home in record time, I unlock my door. I have five minutes before he calls, and I need to get my phone on the charger ASAP.

The first thing I notice amiss is the lights are on. I turned them off. I'm always adamant about turning off lights, so I know something is going on. Taking a couple of steps in, the scent I haven't been able to forget since the day I met John hits me. The house always smells like that cologne, and it drives me wild. Just today, I had to spray some, so it would keep me company, but there's no way it's still that strong. Shaking my head at the absurdity of the situation, I head into the hallway. I must be more tired than I feel.

Dropping my bag on the floor, I look up and have to blink twice, unsure if I'm seeing this shit right or if I've fallen down some crazy rabbit hole. My fiancé is in front of me, and he's in his birthday suit except for a gift box strategically hiding a different kind of package. This man is seriously holding a dick-in-a-box, and I don't know if I want to laugh, run away, or jump him.

"Um…what do you think you're doing?" I ask, trying hard to contain my need to grin.

"I've come to give you your Christmas delivery. It's been sitting here waiting for you to claim it."

"Isn't it a little late for Christmas presents?"

"Not in the North Pole. Besides, I had this specially marked for you. You should have been here hours ago. Aren't you going to open it? I figured this is subtle enough to tell you how much I missed you." He points to the gift-wrapped box with his unoccupied hand. "Dick-in-a-Box."

"Subtle? You don't have a subtle bone in your body," I say, grabbing my bag from the floor and moving past him to the kitchen. I want to see how far he'll take this. From the corner of my eye, I watch him follow me, that ridiculous box making him walk funny. I can't take it anymore and laugh so hard I almost choke from the cough.

He doesn't miss a beat. "Shouldn't my cock be in your mouth when you make that sound?"

The fact that he read my mind has me turning to face him. The box is now on the floor. Unable to stop myself, my eyes shift to 'his delivery.' Fuck, did I miss it and him. My mouth waters at the sight of his long, thick, and obscenely aroused cock. His tip leaks precum, and I instinctively lick my lips, a groan escaping me.

"You really should have told me you were coming home early. I have all these plans and worksheets I have to finish," I say, knowing how bad I'm teasing him right now.

"On your knees, Kent," he demands, with a raw, gruff edge to his tone I hadn't heard before. "The only thing you have to finish is sucking this cock." The way he demands I obey him makes my own arousal ache from the constraints of my pants.

Needing relief, my whole plan to torture him falls to the wayside, and I go to my knees. Wrapping my hand around his length, I stroke it a few times as more precum comes out. I roll my tongue over the small slit, the first taste hitting me, and it tastes so fucking good. The hitch in his breath combined with the hiss he lets out drives me forward, and I wrap my lips around his length.

His hand runs through my hair, grasping it. Taking over, he pushes himself farther into my mouth as I hollow my cheeks.

"Fuck, Kent, that mouth," he grunts out.

Taking him all the way to the back of my throat, I feel his body shudder. He's on the edge of losing control, and I want him there. His grasp tightens, becoming almost punishing, and he thrusts into me faster. He moans, the guttural noises coming from deep inside him, filling me with pleasure. Needing my own relief, I undo my pants, pulling out my cock and stroking it. His cum drips out of my mouth and down my beard, making a mess of it, and I know I'll have his scent there.

His thighs stiffen, almost as if he's trying to cement his balance. I cup the back of his ass, feeling his muscles contract. He's about to release, and I'm greedy for it. Rubbing my own length faster, squeezing as I do, I join him.

"Fuck… Fuck… Fuck! That fucking mouth is going to be the fucking death of me. I'm going to come down your throat, and you're going to take it. Then I'm going to own your tight ass, and you're going to let me. Aren't you, Kent?"

I nod my response and let the word "yes" vibrate from my mouth. I want to see this man begging for his release, knowing I have the power to bring him there.

"Fuck, you're going to unman me right here."

His words are the last push I need as I come on the kitchen floor. John pushes farther, deeper than I thought possible shooting his load as I struggle to swallow it all, some of it spilling out.

Getting up on my feet, I go to button my pants, but his hand stops me, and I look up at him. "Take them off. I'm not done with you," he says, and as if I can't help myself, I do as he wants. He approaches me as I finish shaking off the last pant leg, slamming his mouth on mine in a kiss that's both hot and feral. His hold on my neck is tight, not letting me do anything other than open for him to deepen our kiss. The taste of himself on my tongue has him moaning aloud.

Our fight for dominance continues when I push him up against the wall. Closing the already small gap between us, my cock rubbing against him, the friction causing me to get hard again. That always happens when we're together, never getting enough of each other. I land a hard smack on his ass, causing him to push even further into me.

In a swift motion, he turns us so I'm now against the wall. "Don't fucking deny me when I come home. I went half-crazy stopping myself from marching up to your office and taking you right there. And I still plan to do that one of these days. I want you to smell us every time you're sitting at that desk, pushing your papers and writing your notes," he rasps against my ear before biting my neck and finally landing on my lips again.

I'm so lost in the kiss, in the way his hard body pushes against my own, and the control he's taken from me, I don't argue. Needing to touch him, I grab for his hard cock and rub it, letting his cum spread on my fingers while I jack him off.

"Fuck, you don't how much you're playing with fire right now, Kent."

"Why don't you show me then?" I reply, needing him just as badly.

Since we came home, it's been like this every night, both of us dead set on showing our love to each other in the most intimate of ways. Some moments, it's loving, and others, it's almost animalistic. It's especially hot when I tell him no or talk smack back at him.

"Fine, I guess I need to show you again why you're mine."

I'm surprised when he lifts me, making me wrap around his thighs. The man is built, but sometimes, his strength amazes me. The look in his eyes says my back talk is about to land me good and fucked.

He carries me into the bedroom, and he drops me on the bed. His mouth is on mine again as he climbs over me.

"I was going half-mad today. All I kept thinking about was this, coming home and making love to you," he says between kisses. I'm barely able to tell him I missed him too when he grips my cock, running his hand up and down it.

"Tell me you need it."

"I need it, John. Fuck me."

He reaches over, grabbing the KY from the drawer and pouring it on me as he drives a finger in while he continues to stroke me. Gradually, he pushes another in, fucking me with them. Within minutes, I'm moaning, asking for him to put me out of my misery. I need more — the intimate touches, the way he kisses parts of my body when he does, all of it. Our connection is more than just a carnal need between two bodies. It's a unison of souls.

He pushes his tip into me slowly as he stretches me. The man is huge, and even with all the prepping he did, it still takes him a little bit, but he finally goes in all the way to the hilt. A few slow thrusts at first, then he quickens until he can't control himself. The way he takes me has me ruined in more ways than one, and I'm glad because there will only ever be him. The intimacy between us is a feeling I've never experienced before.

"Holy fuck, John. You're killing me," I cry out, a moan rumbling out of my chest. I prop myself onto my elbows, and our mouths meet once more. The kiss is hungry, more erratic, building a throbbing ache inside me. The whole house is silent except for his grunts, my moans and the sounds of our bodies making contact.

"Stroke yourself. I want you to come all over while I fill you full of me," he demands through gritted teeth, looking me dead in the eyes. He spreads me wider, my legs bent at the knees, and I obey. My own body is at the point of insanity from all the pleasure he's giving me. Making quick work of my length, I feel his release fill my ass, making the fit impossibly tighter, and hear him growl out in pleasure, making me do the same. His name echoes through the walls as I spill all over myself just as he wanted.

When we're both spent, he pulls me to him, my back to his front, his arm possessively around my middle. Laying his head in the crook of my neck, kissing it, he professes his undying love to me like every other night. All is right in our world as we fall asleep. He really is my Christmas delivery.

Epilogue One

~ Kent ~

One Year After Meeting

The last couple of weeks have been hell without my John. These trips always seem to take forever, but duty called. I was sent to a conference to help with the toy designs, my newfound calling. Who would have thought I'd love that aspect so much? While I'd enjoyed working with Grace while she came up with her concepts, I never considered it my career.

The only part of my job I hate are these trips, mostly because they take me away from my better half. Although we call each other every night, it isn't the same. Thankfully, I won't have to take another for months.

Counting the minutes until I get there, I can't wait to be home. I miss John's arms around me, the feel of his chest against my back when we sleep, and most of all, I miss his kisses. Especially the loving way he's always so eager to see me at the end of a long shift. He's come a long way since the day we met, going as far as opening up to those around us and even dishing out the occasional hug without being forced into it.

Speed walking to our home, I don't see his car waiting for me like usual, and an uneasy feeling creeps into the pit of my stomach.

Maybe, something came up.

After all, it's the craziest time of the year. Convincing myself that's the reason, I hum along to the song in my head. As I walk past the town buildings, the fact they're mostly closed faintly registers, but not enough to make me question it. My brain is focused solely on getting to him.

With a one-track mind, I reach the door, unlocking it and yelling out, "I'm home." The place is suspiciously dark, and he is nowhere to be seen. After checking every room, and finding no evidence of life, or that he's been here at all today, I start to panic. Where could he be? Is he okay? Was there an accident at the warehouse?

All these questions run around my head, and I try to not let my anxiety get the best of me. Realizing he's probably at Molly's place, I pick up the phone and call him. No answer. I call my two besties. No answer. I call the head honcho himself. Fucking nothing. That's when worry really starts to set in. I walk frantically out the door and see the note sticking on it that I must have missed on the way here. John's unmistakable penmanship directs me to the Claus' home.

In all of my thirty-one years, I've never felt fear quite like I am right now, not even when I ended up in the hospital after getting hit by a car at fifteen. The more I think about it, the more it dawns on me something is very wrong. Last night, John didn't answer, either, but I figured it was due to the late hour. Grabbing the keys to the car John bought me last month, I head to the main residence.

The whole ride, I'm dialing his number over and over. This time, I don't miss the empty shops as I go by. It's a fucking ghost town. Not even parked cars are on the street. My twisted mind starts spinning some crazy ideas, all of which send me into a moment of insanity. The craziest of them grips my throat, making it hard to breathe.

What if this has all been a dream, and tomorrow, I'll wake up in that Florida apartment, living my humdrum life without my reason for living? The mere idea has my body feeling heavy. I need to get there fast, or I'll be sitting on the side of the road fighting down a panic attack. I can't fathom a day where I don't see his smiling face or we don't sit side by side on the porch at the end of the workday.

"Fuck, I can't do this," I whisper to myself. Just as I'm about to pull over, the house comes into view, and I speed to the driveway. I manage to get out of the car, but I can't bring myself to enter or knock on the door.

How stupid am I being right now?

I stand there, my hand shaking, unable to let it make contact with the doorknob, unaware of how much time passes. Suddenly, I see it open, and there's John Alexander, dressed in one of those tailored suits that always makes me a little weak. It removes all the anxiety as I pull him into a hug.

"Baby, are you okay?" he whispers, holding me tight until I finally let go enough to face him. He cups my cheek, and a tear threatens to fall from my eye. *He's still here. It wasn't some warped dream.*

"I thought, oh God, it's stupid."

"No, it's not. Tell me what's wrong?" He stares into my soul with that patient but demanding demeanor he carries himself with.

"I didn't see anyone, and then the note… I let anxiety get the best of me. For a minute, I thought it was all a dream. As if life was playing a cruel joke on me, and I'd wake up without you once I opened that door."

"Shit, I didn't see it that way, but I can promise that will never happen because…" John says, pulling me down the steps of the house and toward the back, without finishing his sentence.

The suspense is killing me. I open my mouth to demand he finish when I come face-to-face with everyone in the North Pole.

"I want to spend the rest of my life loving you. Waking up to you in my arms and creating our own magic. The last few weeks prove how much I need you to be my husband. God forbid something happens on one of those trips, and I am unable to get to you. So, we're getting married today. In front of all the people who love us."

His words stun me into silence, and my eyes focus on the way his fingers are shaking, his hand out, waiting for me to take it and follow him to our forever.

"Kent?" he asks when I don't answer right away.

"Fuck, sorry…yes, let's do this. I fucking love you."

He wraps his fingers tightly around mine as we go down to the altar, our friends clapping enthusiastically.

"You almost gave me a heart attack there while I waited for you to take my hand. I was for sure you were going to back out of marrying me.

"Hey, gotta keep you on your toes."

We share another kiss before finally taking our spots at the front, facing each other. Standing there in a ridiculously large magistrate robe is Crystal, who's very pregnant and cranky. She's due any minute, so seeing her here, trying to officiate is surprising.

"Okay fuckers, can we get on with this? Seeing as I brought you two together, I feel like you owe me an apology. You had to wait this long to say I do? I'm about to pop, but I wasn't missing this for the world," she says, placing her hand on her belly for emphasis.

"Hey, I tried hinting, but like always, this one doesn't take hints too well," John apologizes.

"Whatever. Just hush so we can get this show on the road," she reprimands.

The ceremony goes quickly, with us saying our own vows. There isn't a dry eye in the place, even from some of the men, who are trying to hide it by coughing into their sleeves. Except for Tony who's letting the tears run freely. When Crystal says kiss the groom, I pull John to me by the back of his neck. Our kiss is passionate, full of possession and all the emotions we have for one another.

"Shit, it's happening."

Crystal's curse word has us stopping mid-kiss. We look over, and she's pointing at the floor, horrified at the puddle of water at her feet.

"Joe Claus, I'm going to fucking kill you! I'm about to pop this baby right here," she yells.

Joe stands from the pew, running then falling on his way, in full panic mode. "Shit, baby, the baby. What…? I…" He's stumbling over his words so badly it's almost comical. I'd laugh if I wasn't worried about my friend. Crystal starts screaming louder than I've ever heard her scream in my life.

"Okay, everyone calm down. Someone get me a wheelchair from my dad's room." Brandie spins into action, directing all of us. "Joe, stop freaking out, and go get the bag you brought just in case. It's in the closet. And you two." She points at us. "For heaven's sake, don't just stand there. Get the car ready, we're going to have a baby, and it's coming in fast."

John runs, pulling the car onto the back lawn, and Joe ushers her into it. I take the passenger seat, wanting to be there for her. On the way to our medical center, the scene playing out in the back of the car is one for the books.

"I promise you, next time you try to put that dick in me, I'm going to tear it off!" Crystal says. It's followed by a yelp from him, causing me to glance backward.

"You don't mean that, honey. It's the baby talking," he says, making the mistake of uttering the wrong words. Crystal let's go of his hand and grabs his junk for emphasis, making me hurt just from seeing it.

"Try me! I'm not kidding! 'Oh, it'll be good, baby. Oh, you know you want this candy cane.' That candy cane is what caused this." She glares at him.

I convince her to pull away her hand before she causes real damage, and Joe mouths a thank you in my direction.

Three hours later, we welcome Joe Claus, Jr. and Brandie Grace Claus, on the same day I got my forever. This place is definitely magical, and we have another Christmas delivery.

Epilogue Two

~ John Alexander ~

Two Years After That — February 1st

Looking at my clock again, I grow impatient. *Where is he?* My husband should be here already, keeping all the crazy Cupids away from me. I love them, but they can be overwhelming as hell. Especially since they're in wedding mode. To say they're a colorful bunch is putting it mildly, all except, Romeo. He's the oldest and only still-single child in the Cupid clan, and he gets reminded of it at every turn.

"Oh, John, I'm so happy you came. I didn't see you last year with that handsome husband of yours," Lovin Cupid, Romeo's mom, greets me, pulling at my cheeks like she used to do when I was a child.

Yeah, Kent is going to be in trouble.

"I wouldn't miss it for the world, especially since it said mandatory on the invitation," I say as politely as I can. The woman is a bit crazy, and has made sure her children get married off as soon as possible. Except for Romeo, her sore spot.

"Well, I had to make sure everyone was here for my daughter's rehearsal dinner. Speaking of everyone, where's that precious Crystal? Too bad I didn't scoop her up, first. She would have been perfect for Romeo, that stubborn child of mine," she says, before walking away, not waiting for an answer.

This isn't the first time she's made that comment, and if it wasn't because Romeo's made it very clear, Crystal is his cousin's wife, and that's just sick. I'm sure Joe would be breaking down the Cupid empire. Especially since Crystal is pregnant again, and she's been sicker this time around. He's been grunting at the anything that moves the wrong way at his woman.

With a sigh of relief, I see Kent come through the door. Behind him is a pissed-off looking Romeo. I really feel for the guy. It can't be easy dealing with a mother who's trying to get you hitched at every breathing moment.

"Yo, Romeo, what's up?" I ask him, pulling him into a side hug. We're good friends. On Saturdays, we all shoot pool and talk shop, comparing holiday traffic.

Turning to my husband, I give him a quick kiss. "Took you long enough. I've already been visited by the Cupid matriarch. I thought I'd have to fake death, and even then, I think she'd try and spin it into a tragic love story."

Kent laughs at my comment, but Romeo grunts. "You ain't kidding. I made him wait for me. That's why we were late. I wasn't coming here alone and unchaperoned. The more barriers between me and my mother the better. She's gotten it into her head that I'm going to be engaged by my sister's wedding," he says, looking around nervously.

"She was making a case for you stealing Joe's girl."

"That again?" Kent asks, and I nod.

"She's determined to get me engaged by my sister's wedding because my being single is bad for business."

"It is, and I've found you someone already," his mother says, coming up behind us. The look of horror on his face makes me pity him.

"Mom, it's not happening. I don't need a date. I got it covered."

"Oh yeah, and how might that be? You won't show up without a date for the wedding. I've already called the Lantern's. Their daughter is single and pretty.

At the mention of Sonja Lantern, I see him shudder. Those two are like siblings, and I already know this won't go over well with either one of them. He looks over at me, eyes begging for an out, and I know I'll have to pull this out of my ass.

"He doesn't need one. Romeo's been dating a friend of mine, but she's a very reserved person, so he was keeping it quiet. You know how that goes, but I'm sure she wouldn't be happy to know you're trying to set him up," I say quickly, trying to cover for my friend, who looks as surprised as his mother.

"Oh my god! This is the best news ever! I have to go tell your sister, no your father, hell, I'm telling everyone!" With that, she spins on her heel and is off.

"Dude, what the fuck? Now, what am I going to do? I don't have a date!"

"Actually, I know the perfect girl," I say, causing Kent to quirk an eyebrow. "My friend is saving up to leave town, and I'm pretty sure she'll help you with your situation for the right price."

"Right price?"

"Yeah, a thousand bucks."

"A thousand bucks?" they both yell out in unison

"Hey, you're the desperate one, not me. She'll do you a favor and disappear the next day. Besides, she's super sweet, and your mother will love her," I tell him, knowing he'll end up sticking to my plan.

"Is this her thing, like an escort?" Romeo asks obviously uncomfortable.

"No, but she's already done every odd job she could find, from fixing computers to plumbing. Even with all that and working at the diner, she still needs a couple thousand more before she has enough to leave. I'm sure she'd be willing, as long as you don't try anything."

"Shit, fine, can you call her? I'm really desperate."

Signaling him to wait, I dial the number and wait for an answer. "Chels, hey, it's me John…" I walk away, but Kent's eyes never leave me. He knows what I'm up to. I'm trying to play Cupid, hoping it doesn't blow up in my face.

Returning after a few minutes, I give him the good news. "Okay, you got yourself a date. She'll go to all the pre-wedding events, but she's not buying anything fancy, so if it's required, you'll have to buy it.

"Fair enough. When do I meet her so we can go over our story," Romeo says, turning to his usual business attitude.

"Tomorrow at *The Lounge*. She'll be at the last table in the dimly lit corner," I say, ready to head out of this party.

"I feel like I'm hiring a hitman."

"In a sense, you are," Kent replies, knowing exactly who I set him up with.

"What's that supposed to mean?"

"I got to go. Be there!" I tell him, taking my husband's arm and exiting the party.

Kent waits until Romeo is out of sight before laying into me. "Chels? Really? You know damn well those two will clash."

"Or fall in love. You never know."

"You're playing with fire, but that's going to be on you. I didn't realize how sneaky you've been lately, trying to pair people up."

"I blame it on you. I want everyone to be as happy as we are," I say, kissing his shoulder. "I've been missing you so much. I can't wait to get home, so we can soak in the bathtub. I'm sure you're tired, and I can give you a massage." This time, he was gone for three weeks, and I really missed him more than usual.

"I missed you, too." He stops right outside our car and pulls me to him for a kiss.

He's my home, my haven, my whole world. Laying my forehead against his, I wrap my arms around his narrow waist. "Don't ever be gone that long again. My heart can't take it. Next time, I'm coming with you, and I'll sit through all those horrible meetings I know you hate."

"Deal, because I was dying without you," he tells me, helping calm my need just a bit.

Just as promised, the next trip he takes, I'm right there with him. And as for Romeo… Let's just say, he may have gotten more than he bargained for.

About the Author

Most days you can find Pixie running around trying to juggle 100 hats…one of which is Author. BTW, she still can't believe that's what she gets to call herself that. What started out as a passion for book blogging turned into publishing her very first novella… *Sealed With A Kiss.*

Pixie who is part of the LGBT Community, writes MF and FF stories that are sexy, insta-love stories full of heart and with a HEA.

Her characters not only fall quickly, deeply, but are also possessive in nature. If she's not writing, then she's on Facebook…Tell her to get the hell out of there and get writing.

"Where Love Always Wins."

You can follow Pixie Chica via any of the social media by clicking the link below:
https://linktr.ee/pixiechica

Books by Pixie

Always & Forever Series
Sealed with a Kiss
In Plain Sight

Love Unexpected Series
Love at Sunset
Undeniable Love
Unleashed Love

Valladares Family Saga
Ivy's Rebellion

Tattooed Brides Series
Loved by Her
Loved in the Dark

Lancaster Falls Series
Because of Blue
Because of You

Holiday Hearts
Mistletoe
Undercover Santa
His Christmas Delivery
Stupid Cupid
Altared

Sweetville
Put a Ring on It
Stranded Christmas
Ring of Fire
Good Cop Bad Girl
Happenstance

Latimer Ladies
New Year's Kiss
Sweetness
Last Shot

Price Industries
Mine by Christmas
Give into Temptation

Sizzle Beach
Things We Did Last Summer

Standalones
A Wolfe's Ruby
A Royal Payne
Treat You Better
Teacher's Pet
Playing for Keeps
Curves Rx
My Vampire Mate

Box Sets
Holiday Hearts Collection
The Covingtons
Price Industries